C0-ASD-996

The Jungle
Goes Bananas

BILL CONDON

Illustrated by Geoff Hocking

Triple3Play

sundance

A Haights Cross Communications Company

Published by
Sundance Publishing
P.O. Box 740
One Beeman Road
Northborough, MA 01532
800-343-8204

Copyright © text Bill Condon 2001
Copyright © illustrations Geoff Hocking 2001

First published 2001 as Supa Dazzlers by
Pearson Education Australia Pty Limited
95 Coventry Street
South Melbourne 3205 Australia
Exclusive United States Distribution: Sundance Publishing

ISBN 0-7608-6178-1

Contents

*For Victoria McGuinness and her friends
at St. Joseph's School, Bulli*

Chapter 1

Dad's Masterpiece

Once there was a very clever girl named Kendra who had very creative parents.

Kendra's mom Mavis was a very famous person. She invented Vanishing Cream. But she disappeared a long time ago. So she won't be talked about again in this story.

Kendra's father's name was Cyril. Kendra didn't like that name very much, so she called him Dad.

All of his life, Dad had been a tree surgeon. Sadly, on a very windy day, one of his patients fell on him.

Dad logged off from the tree doctor business. He looked around for another job. He remembered all of the fun that Mavis had as an inventor. So he decided to become one, too.

And he was very good at it!

Dad came up with one idea that he called Glow-in-the-Dark-Babies. It helped mothers find their babies in the dark.

When his neighbor's cat had itchy places that it couldn't reach, Dad invented the Automatic Cat Back-Scratcher.

And to impress Kendra, Dad invented a new way to fly. But it still needed a little work.

It was true that these inventions were a little rough, but Dad kept trying. And he kept getting better. Then he began making his masterpiece. For months, he worked hard in his lab on a very secret invention.

"What is it, Dad?" asked Kendra.

"It's your birthday present," he replied.

"Is it an instant chocolate-making machine?"

"No, Kendra."

"Is it a machine that will do my homework for me?"

"No, Kendra."

"OK, Dad. I give up. What is it?"

"Be patient," he said. "It will be finished by 5 A.M. Then all will be revealed!"

Chapter 2

An Amazing Present

Kendra was out of bed the next morning even before the sun came up. She raced to Dad's lab and flung open the door just as the clock struck 5 A.M.

"Happy birthday!" said Dad. "This is your present."

Dad gave a silly grin and patted the tall, shiny box beside him.

It was big enough to hold two people. Inside were two chairs, two safety belts, two crash helmets, and two switches.

One switch said BACK. The other one said FORWARD. A tiny screen that showed the year was beside the switches.

"It's cool," said Kendra. "Really cool. But what is it?"

"A time machine, of course."

"Wow!"

Kendra flipped over backward and did cartwheels around the lab. "Gee, thanks!" she said. "Just what I've always wanted!"

"Me, too," replied Dad. "Now we can travel backward and forward in time. But there's more. It also has a laboratory."

He flicked a button, and the floor slowly opened to reveal another room. It was a compact room that had tall shelves lining its walls. Piled on the shelves was every item an inventor could ever hope for. The room was also equipped with a fancy new computer.

"Now wherever we go, I can help people with my inventions," Dad said.

The more Kendra thought about zipping around in time, the more she liked it. She could take her friends out in the time machine. They'd like that.

Kendra even thought that she could bring back some creature from the past to keep as a pet. A real dinosaur—perhaps, like a baby T-rex!

"So what are we waiting for?" said Dad. "Let's see if it works!"

Dad jumped into the time machine, but Kendra hung back.

"Not so fast," she said. "You mean you haven't tested it yet?"

"No, not yet. But I'm certain it will work. The only problem is that we won't know exactly where we'll be going. And I don't know if it will explode. Other than that, there are no problems."

Kendra knew that Dad was going to try the time machine no matter what. She couldn't let him go on his own. Besides, she thought it might be fun—as long as they survived!

"OK," she said. "I'm game if you are."

"Jump in and shut the door!" Dad shouted. "It's time to blast off!"

Chapter 3

Screaming Through Time

Seat belts were fastened. Helmets were strapped on tightly.

Dad flipped a coin. "Heads we go back in time. Tails we go forward." The coin sailed up high, spinning and spinning, and came down . . . HEADS. "Let's do it!" yelled Dad.

The time machine groaned into life as Dad pressed the BACK button. It sounded like an elephant with a tuskache!

"Maybe this isn't such a good idea," said Kendra. "Maybe we should just get a video about time travel. Maybe . . ."

WHOOSHHHHH!

There were bright lights. Red, green, orange, and the deepest blue.

There were loud echoes. And hissing whispers.

They were in dark, dim tunnels.
They were in a blinding light.

They were flying.

They were sinking.

They were screaming!

The lid has been removed so you can see what is happening (for this drawing only).

YiKES!

Suddenly the year 1836 appeared on the tiny screen. And then . . . *BOINNNGGG! BOINNNGGG! BOINNNGGG!* The time machine bounced up high, hit the ground, and bounced straight back up again.

"What's happening?" wailed Kendra.

"I wanted to avoid crash landings," Dad replied calmly. "So the base of the time machine is one huge spring."

"Good thinking, Dad! But how do you make it stop bouncing?"

"It stops itself after six bounces," Dad replied.

"Excellent," said Kendra.

"Then it hovers about 20 feet above the ground. We can use the ladder to climb down."

"What ladder, Dad?"

"Uh-oh," he said. "I knew I forgot something."

Kendra peered out the window. They were in the middle of a jungle. All around them were the sounds of birds screeching and wild animals roaring. It seemed dangerous and scary, but they couldn't stay up in the time machine forever.

"Come on, Dad," Kendra said, as she opened the top. "We'll jump down."

The brave adventurers climbed out of the time machine and leaped into the jungle. But instead of landing in long grass, they tumbled into something very wet and warm.

"Oh, no!" shouted Kendra. "We're going to be cooked and eaten."

"There's no need to panic," Dad told her. "We're not tied up. We can just get out of this pot and walk away."

But when they tried to get out, they found that they were stuck. It wasn't water in the pot. It was some gooey stuff, and it had them trapped.

"Oh dear! What do we do now?" asked Kendra nervously.

"Well," Dad replied thoughtfully. "When the owners of the pot arrive, we should try to convince them to only eat fruit."

Chapter 4

Toezan, King of the Bungle

Seconds later, they heard someone approaching. Dad glanced at his watch. It was 12 o'clock. Lunchtime!

A man stepped out of the jungle. He was tall and skinny, and if he had any muscles, he'd left them at home. He must have left his hair at home, too, because his head looked exactly like a bowling ball. Only there were no holes for your fingers.

He was a funny-looking man, and he looked even funnier because his clothes. They were made out of banana skins!

"Great galloping giraffes!" he said when he spotted Dad and Kendra. "What are you two doing in my oatmeal?"

Kendra wanted to say, "The backstroke." But she knew it wasn't a good idea to tell corny jokes—especially when she was in a cooking pot! So she said nothing.

But as it turned out, the funny-looking man was really quite nice. Once he learned that the pair were not oatmeal thieves, he helped them out of the pot. He even gave them a free bowl of his gooey food.

Dad and Kendra introduced themselves, and the man smiled and shook their hands.

"I suppose you've heard of Starzan, King of the Jungle?" he asked.

"Of course we have."

"Well, I'm his son, Toezan, King of the Bungle."

"Really?" said Dad.

"Truly?" said Kendra.

"Yes. Really and truly."

Then Toezan told them his whole sad story.

Starzan could swing on vines from tree to tree while beating his chest with his free hand and yelling very loudly. He could also out-wrestle wild animals and swim faster than the fastest crocodile.

He expected that his only son would be exactly like him.

WRONG!

Just the thought of wild animals made Toezan tremble.

When he swung on vines, something always got in his way.

And he had the oddest swimming style. It was called drowning.

"I'm such a loser," Toezan said. "Everyone in the jungle calls me King of the Bungle. And that's what I am—a failure!"

Chapter 5

The Princess Problem

Dad was so excited to hear about Toezan's problems that he did a handstand.

Kendra put her hand over her face. Parents could be *so* embarrassing!

"Are you feeling OK?" Toezan asked Dad.

"Yes! I'm just happy, that's all," Dad said.

"You're happy because I'm a failure?"

"No! I'm happy because I can make you a winner!" laughed Dad.

"How?" asked Toezan.

Dad quickly explained about the time machine and his many other inventions.

"I promise you I can invent some things that will change your life," Dad said.

Toezan blinked and shook his head.

"You'll have to slow down a little. I'm still thinking about that great invention you just told me about."

"You mean the time machine?"

"No. I mean the Back-Scratcher for cats. You must be a genius!"

"You bet your bananas he is!" said Kendra.

Toezan hopped about in delight.

"Leaping Lions!" he shouted. "I'm ready when you are. Go ahead and make me a winner, Mr. Inventor!"

Dad said that first he needed to find out exactly what Toezan wanted most of all.

"That's easy," Toezan answered. "I want to marry Lah-Loo—the woman I love!"

"Tell me more," said Dad.

Toezan explained that Lah-Loo loved him, too. But an ancient family rule did not allow her to marry him.

"What rule is that?" asked Kendra.

"Never marry a fool," Toezan replied.

"Oh, *that* rule!"

"Yes. Lah-Loo is a princess. The king and queen will only allow us to marry if I swing though the trees without crashing into things and out-wrestle wild animals. They also expect me to be a great swimmer, instead of a great drowner!"

Dad grinned so hard his face almost broke.

"Leave it to me, Toezan," he said. "Lah-Loo will soon be yours!"

Chapter 6

Monkey Madness!

One look above him told Dad why Toezan always hit things when he swung through the trees. There were dozens of monkeys swinging in dozens of directions, all at the same time. It was monkey madness!

Dad grabbed a lift on a passing giraffe and climbed into the time machine. He pressed the button that opened the lab. In just a few minutes, he made a red **STOP** sign and a green **Go** sign. He quickly fitted them with lights, a camera, and a timer. Then he slid down the neck of the giraffe and landed at Toezan's feet.

"Here you go," he smiled. "Just what this jungle needs—traffic lights!"

It was a clever idea. But even Toezan knew that monkeys wouldn't obey traffic lights.

"The lights aren't for the monkeys," Dad said. "They're for you, Toezan. When there's a break in the vine traffic, the green light will come on. Then you'll know that it's safe for you to go."

"Raging rhinos!" whooped Toezan. "Perfect!"

Dad placed the traffic lights high up in the roof of the jungle. Then Kendra went and got Lah-Loo and the king and queen.

As soon as Lah-Loo arrived, Toezan blew his sweetheart a kiss.

"I love you," she gushed.

"I love you, too," he gushed right back.

"This is too much," grunted the king.

"Get on with the vine-swinging," snapped the queen.

"Ring-a-ding-ding!" yelled Toezan. "Watch me swing!"

With that, he scrambled up a tree, grabbed a vine, and sailed merrily through the air.

He swung high. He swung low. He beat his chest with his free hand and yelled very loudly.

"At last," cried Toezan, "I'm a winner."

But then, as four monkeys suddenly appeared directly in front of him, he remembered something very important. He was color-blind!

CLUNK!

CLUNK!

CLUNK!

CLUNK!

A Lovesick Gorilla

The king and queen were not impressed. No matter what she said, they would not let their daughter marry Toezan. To them, he was still the biggest bungler in the jungle.

"What would make you change your mind?" Dad asked the king and queen.

"If Toezan can out-wrestle Gertie, the fiercest gorilla in the jungle, we might allow it," said the queen.

Dad grinned. "No problem. Be here tomorrow morning. Toezan will wrestle Gertie—and win!"

Toezan's knees clanged together, his jaw shook, and even his ears trembled.

"Th-th-that's right," he stuttered. "I'm v-v-very sure that I'll beat th-th-that big, hairy gorilla."

Then he fainted.

Dad and Kendra worked hard all that night. By morning, they had invented the world's first gorilla repellent! "One whiff of this, and Gertie will run away," said Dad.

"Are you sure this will work?" Toezan asked Kendra, while she was busy spraying him with repellent.

"What could go wrong?" said Dad cheerfully.

"Oh . . . Gertie could squeeze him to death," replied Kendra. "Or tear him into little pieces. Or she could sit on him for about two years!"

Toezan fainted. Again!

Soon all was ready for the wrestling match.

Lah-Loo blew Toezan a kiss. The king and queen frowned. Gertie, the biggest, wildest gorilla in the jungle, **ROARED!**

Toezan tried to run away, but Gertie pounced on him. She swept him above her head and whirled him around and around.

Gertie was about to toss Toezan onto the ground and stomp on him. But then, a strange look appeared on her face.

"The repellent's taking effect," whispered Dad. "She'll run away in a second."

Kendra wasn't quite so sure because she'd just remembered a well-known fact.

If you use too much repellent, it becomes an attractant!

Gertie gently lowered Toezan to the ground. She tilted her head from side to side, and then she winked at him!

Just then, a pack of lovesick gorillas thundered out of the jungle. They all headed straight for Toezan!

Chapter 8

Impossible?

Toezan ran faster than any human being had ever run before. He didn't stop until he dived into a lake and washed away every drop of gorilla repellent.

The king and queen laughed and hooted, "That fool will never marry our daughter now!"

"What would change your mind?" asked Dad.

The king pointed to the Mighty Munchie River—full of crocodiles! "If Toezan can cross the river, he may marry Lah-Loo."

"But that's impossible!" Lah-Loo cried. "Toezan will be eaten by the river's crocs."

"And I can't swim! That makes it even more impossible," added Toezan.

Dad had no idea how he could help Toezan cross the river. But he couldn't just stand back and watch. He had to do something!

"It *is* possible!" Dad said. "That tiny river is nothing to Toezan. And as for the crocodiles . . . he'll turn them into handbags if they so much as look at him."

Kendra tugged at Dad's sleeve. "Be careful!" she warned. But Dad wasn't listening.

"Come here tomorrow morning," he told the king and queen. "You can watch Toezan swim the Mighty Munchie River. Not once, not twice, but three times!"

The king rubbed his hands together. "We'll be here all right," he said. "There's nothing better than watching crocs eat their breakfast!"

Chapter 9

Kendra to the Rescue

As usual, Dad came up with lots of good ideas. The best one was the Hippo-tow.

"That will get me across the river," said Toezan. "But it won't stop me from being eaten."

Toezan water-skis behind two hippos.

So Dad went back to the lab and came up with one of his greatest inventions ever.

"Try these on," he said, holding up shorts that had a rocket attached to them.

"It's a wonderful idea," said Toezan, but he looked very worried.

During this time, Kendra had been working quietly on her own idea. She was a pretty good inventor herself.

"I'm finished!" she exclaimed, just as morning arrived.

She had used some things in Dad's lab to make a lifelike rubber model of Toezan.

"Listen closely," she said. "The model is only part of the plan. I also have a secret weapon!"

A large crowd waited by the river to see Toezan jump into the Mighty Munchie.

"I love you!" sobbed Lah-Loo.

"I love you, too!" Toezan sobbed right back.

"Bring on the crocodiles!" shouted the king and queen.

The crowd cheered as Toezan splashed into the river. About twenty hungry crocodiles splashed in after him.

It was then that Kendra took out her secret weapon. It was a machine that fired fancy chocolates!

POP! POP! POP! POP!

Each time a button on the machine was pressed, dozens of yummy chocolates flew into the crowd. The people went wild! They swept up the chocolates and gobbled them right down.

While everyone was distracted, Toezan leaped out of the water and hid in the long grass. Then Kendra threw the lifelike rubber model into the river. Only now it was equipped with a small, high-speed motor!

Kendra pressed a remote control switch, and the Toezan-model took off. Down the river it went, followed by a bunch of hungry crocs in hot pursuit.

"Wow! Look at that!" screamed the crowd. "Look at Toezan go! What a swimmer! He's amazing!"

"And he's so cute!" sighed Lah-Loo. She waved and blew kisses at the model of Toezan.

"Oh, no!" howled the king. "I don't believe my eyes. This can't be happening!"

"I feel sick!" moaned the queen.

At last Toezan was a winner. Or was he?

Chapter 10

Toezan, King of the Jungle

The rubber model zoomed up and down the river. Toezan waited in the bushes to take the model's place. But on the third trip, a very fast crocodile managed to catch up with the rubber model.

The croc opened its huge jaws around the model's head and went **SNAP!**

Then other crocs caught up, and they all went **SNAP,** too!

Lah-Loo was so upset that she dived into the river and swam toward the crocs.

"You leave my Toezan alone!" she screamed.

"Oh my goodness! My sweetheart is in danger!" cried Toezan.

He forgot that he couldn't swim and that he was afraid of crocodiles. He plunged into the Mighty Munchie River and swam faster than a flying fish. And with every powerful stroke he yowled—very loudly!

It is a well-known fact that the crocodiles of the Mighty Munchie River have really sensitive hearing. Toezan's yowling hurt their ears, so they swam out of the river as fast as they could.

"I love you!" Toezan roared to Lah-Loo. He swept her up in his skinny arms and carried her back to the shore.

"You're my hero!" she cried.

Smiling broadly, Dad approached the king and queen. "Toezan saved your daughter's life. Surely you'll let him marry her now. After all, you've seen how much he loves her and how brave he is."

"No way!" said the king.

"It'll take more than that," added the queen.

"What will it take?" Dad asked.

"I know!" said Kendra.

She held out the chocolate-firing machine. "Will you let them marry if I give you this?"

Kendra pushed the button on the device, and dark, creamy chocolates flew out.

"You've got a deal!" said the king.

"Yum! Yum!" said the queen.

That night Dad and Kendra took part in a double ceremony. The first part of it was the marriage of Toezan and Lah-Loo. In the second part, Toezan was given a new name. From that day on, he was known as Toezan, King of the Jungle!

"We make a good team," said Kendra, as the time machine headed back home. "Do you think that we'll use the time machine again?"

Dad grinned. "You bet your bananas!"

About the Author

Bill Condon

Bill Condon is lucky to be alive. Recently, while working inside his house, he fell off a ladder. He toppled over and fell headfirst into a very large goldfish bowl. He was trapped in that fishbowl for two whole days! If it hadn't been for those goldfish, Bill would have starved to death!

About the Illustrator

Geoff Hocking

Geoff Hocking started illustrating books for children during the 1970s, when he and his wife, Christine, lived and worked in London.

Since then, he has illustrated dozens of books, written some, painted pictures, built a house of mud, spent too much money on foreign cars, and taught design and illustration to hundreds of people.

He and Christine have three children. One is a fashion designer, one is a graphic designer, and one is a preteen who does crazy drawings and worries about losing his hair.